BIBLE HEROES
of the Old Testament

By Christin Ditchfield

Illustrated by Ande Cook

A GOLDEN BOOK • NEW YORK

Copyright © 2004 by Random House, Inc. All rights reserved under International and Pan-American Copyright Conventions. Published in the United States by Golden Books, an imprint of Random House Children's Books, a division of Random House, Inc., New York, and simultaneously in Canada by Random House of Canada Limited, Toronto. Golden Books, A Golden Book, A Little Golden Book, the G colophon, and the distinctive gold spine are registered trademarks of Random House, Inc. Library of Congress Control Number: 2003116087
ISBN 0-375-82816-8
www.goldenbooks.com
Printed in the United States of America   First Random House Edition 2004
20 19 18 17 16 15 14 13

Adam

Adam was the very first person who ever lived.
When the world was still brand-new, God
brought all the animals he had created to Adam.
"Butterfly . . . lion . . . hippopotamus . . . giraffe."
There, in the beautiful Garden of Eden, Adam
gave every creature a name.

Noah

This is Noah, who obeyed God in a time when other men didn't. One day, God told him there would be a terrible flood to wash away all the wickedness on earth. God told Noah to build a great big boat—called an ark—to save his family and all the animals in the world.

After the animals came to Noah, two by two, it began to rain. Soon the whole world was covered with water, but God kept everyone inside the ark safe and dry. Sometimes Noah's family wondered if it would ever stop raining, but Noah trusted God.

One day, the sun came out, and a beautiful rainbow appeared in the sky. The rainbow was God's promise that there would never be a flood like that again.

Joseph

Once there was a boy named Joseph. His father loved him very much. When Joseph's father gave him a beautiful coat of many colors, Joseph's brothers were jealous. They sold him as a slave, far away in Egypt. But God watched over Joseph as he grew up, because he had a plan for him.

One night, Pharaoh, the king of Egypt, had a frightening dream. With God's help, Joseph told Pharaoh that the dream meant hungry times were coming. Joseph said that the king must start to store up food for his people.

The king was very pleased with Joseph's advice. Years later when the dream came true, Joseph had become king! He'd stored up enough food to feed all the people in the land. Now Joseph understood why God had wanted him to live in Egypt. And he forgave his brothers for what they had done to him.

Miriam

Many years later, God's people were living in Egypt. A new ruler forced them to work as slaves. He even sent his soldiers to harm all the newborn boys. When a baby named Moses was born, his mother laid him in a basket and hid it among the reeds by the riverbank.

Moses' big sister, Miriam, was very brave. Day after day, she stood at the edge of the water, keeping watch over Baby Moses. One day, the king's daughter saw the baby in the basket. She felt sorry for him and took him back to the palace to live with her. And Miriam knew that Moses would be safe.

Moses

When Moses grew up, he led God's people out of Egypt, away from the wicked king. But when the king sent his army to capture them and bring them back, the people were trapped between the soldiers and the Red Sea!

Moses knew that God would help his people. So Moses raised his staff. A mighty wind blew, and the waters parted! When the soldiers tried to follow the people, the water came crashing over them. Moses was the greatest leader his people had ever known.

Joshua

After Moses died, Joshua became the leader of God's people. God told Joshua to destroy the wicked city of Jericho—but not with swords or spears. God ordered his people to march around and around the city walls.

The people wondered how they could possibly win a battle just by marching. But Joshua trusted God. When Joshua gave the signal, the people let out a great shout of praise to God. The earth shook—and the city walls came tumbling down!

Samson

Samson was the strongest man in the whole world. When his enemies hid in their great walled city, Samson pulled the city gates right off the hinges. God gave Samson the strength to knock down an entire stadium with one giant push!

Deborah

When God's people had problems, they came to
Deborah. Deborah was a very wise woman. She helped
the people to understand and obey God's commands.

One day, when enemies attacked, the people were terrified. The commander of the army refused to lead his soldiers into battle unless Deborah went with them! So Deborah bravely led the way.

David

Once a shepherd boy named David heard a giant named Goliath cursing God and his people. Though he was just a boy, David went out to fight Goliath all by himself.

The giant laughed when he saw David coming.
But David had prayed that God would guide his hands.
He put a small stone into his slingshot and hurled it
toward Goliath. The stone hit the giant right in the
middle of his forehead—and he fell at David's feet.

As a shepherd boy, David wrote many beautiful songs of praise to God. After he had killed Goliath, David grew up to be a brave and mighty warrior. He sang songs to thank God for giving him victory over his enemies. God was so pleased with David that he made him king over all the people.

Solomon

In time, David's son Solomon became king. God was pleased that Solomon did not pray for riches, but for an understanding heart. God made King Solomon the wisest man who ever lived, and people came from all over the world to listen to his words. They brought him gifts of gold, silver, and precious jewels. King Solomon used these treasures to build a glorious temple where everyone could worship God.

Elijah

Have you heard of Elijah? He listened closely to God and gave God's messages to others. He taught the way of God in a wicked time. And with God's mighty power, Elijah performed many miracles.

When he had finished the work God gave him to do, Elijah was carried into heaven in a chariot of fire.

Esther

Queen Esther was not only beautiful, but brave. One day, she discovered that a wicked man had come up with a plan to destroy all of God's people.

The law said that no one could talk to the king without permission—not even the queen! But Esther went to the king anyway. Bowing low before his throne, she begged him to protect the people. The king listened to Esther. Because she had the courage to speak up, Queen Esther saved the lives of thousands of people.

Daniel

Daniel was the king's closest friend. He helped the king make important decisions. The king's other friends grew jealous of Daniel, so they set a trap for him.

They tricked the king into making a new law: Anyone who didn't pray to the king would be thrown into a den of fierce, hungry lions. The men knew that Daniel would not pray to the king because Daniel prayed only to God. So when Daniel broke the law, he was thrown into the lions' den!

The next morning, the king rushed to the lions' den to see what had happened. He called out, "Daniel, has your God saved you?"

"It's all right, Your Majesty," called Daniel. "God sent his angel to shut the mouths of the lions." Daniel had trusted God. And God had protected Daniel.

Jonah

Do you know the story of Jonah? God had an important job for him, but Jonah didn't want to do it. So he sailed away on a ship and tried to hide from God. But a terrible storm washed Jonah overboard—and then a big fish swallowed him.

Inside the fish, Jonah felt scared and lonely. "Lord," he prayed, "I'm sorry for running away. Please help me!"

Just then, the fish spat Jonah out onto the shore! This time, Jonah did just what God wanted him to do. He traveled to a city called Nineveh and told the people there how to please God. And God was pleased with Jonah.